The
Moon Jet

Written by Roderick Hunt
Illustrated by Nick Schon,
based on the original characters
created by Roderick Hunt and Alex Brychta

OXFORD
UNIVERSITY PRESS

Read these words

moon | soon
cool | shoot
zoom | shoo
boom | food

Kipper had a box and a bin.

Kipper got in his jet . . .

. . . and put on the lid.

“This jet is cool,” said Kipper.

"Off I go," he said.

The jet shot off.

It shot out of the room.

"I will loop the loop,"
said Kipper.

The jet did six loops.

"I will go to the moon,"
said Kipper.

“I can get to it soon,”
he said.

The jet got to the moon.

But the moon bugs ran up.

"Yuk," said Kipper.

"Moon bugs."

“Shoo, get off,” said Kipper.

“Did I nod off?” said Kipper.

“Yes,” said Mum. “Get up to bed.”

Talk about the story

A maze

Help Kipper to get to the moon.

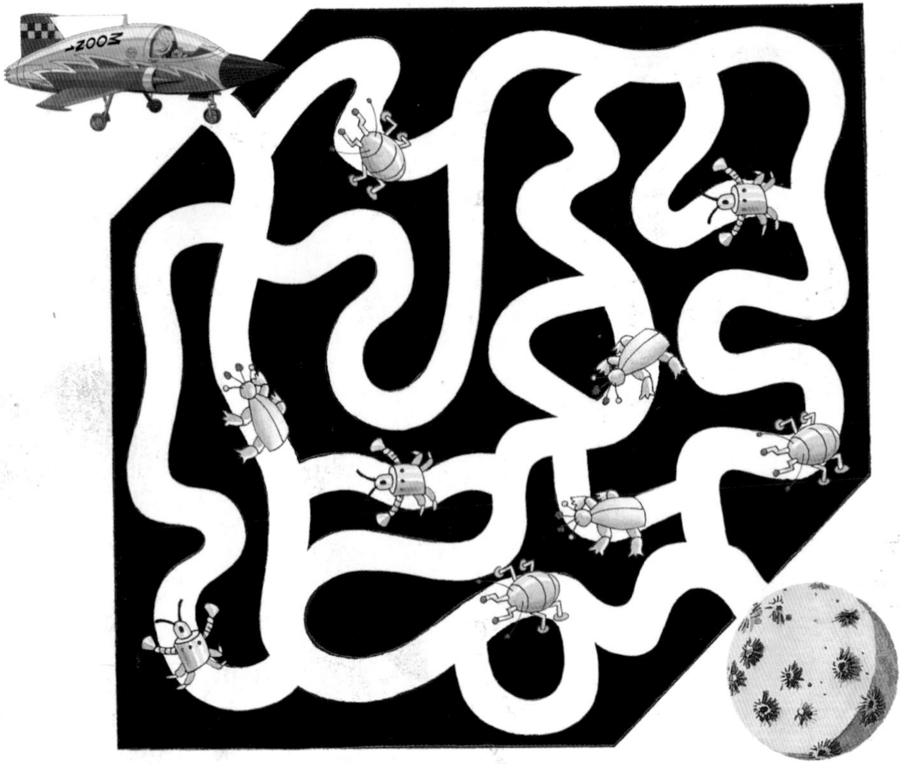